GRIN'S MESSAGE

CARLTON SCOTT

Ends of the Earth Books

ISBN 0-9636652-7-8

Ends of the Earth Books

Also by Carlton Scott: Little Big Wolf

Story and illustrations: Carlton Scott
Editing: Laurie Rosen
Graphic Design: Amy Forret
Printing: Worzalla Publishing

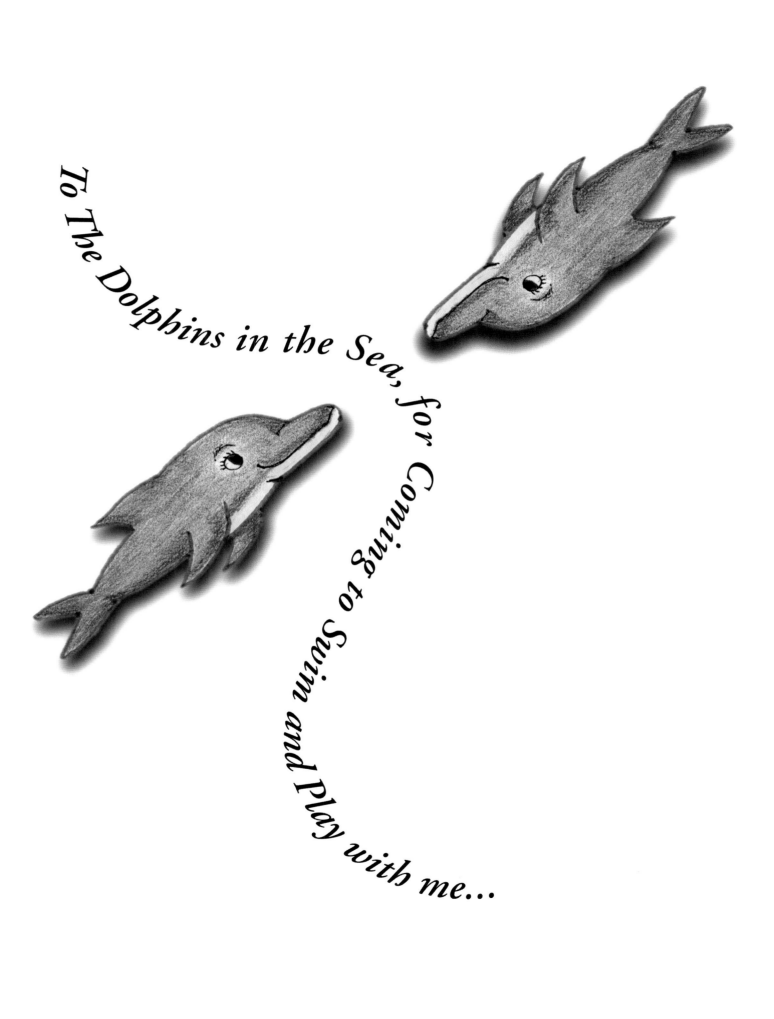

To The Dolphins in the Sea, for Coming to Swim and Play with me...

Off tropical shores, flowing green and blue,
Colorful waters are calling to you.
This story is about my undersea friend:
A bottlenose dolphin, and his name is Grin.

He has a message with a solution:
Grin doesn't fight wars or cause pollution.
He Swims and plays, and greedy he's not.
Grin loves to surf waves and chase fish a lot.

Leaping and flipping, Grin plays a new game,
But someone needs help; their voice calls his name.
Grin hears the yelp, "HELP!" And swims down to see,
An octopus trapped, struggling helplessly.
"Can you please help me?" The octopus moans.
"I'm stuck in the trash between these stones."

"Sure I can help, and save you from harm.
Hold on to my fins, and we'll free your arm.
Don't worry," Grin says reassuringly.
As they tug and tug and pull his arm free.
"Thank you very much for being so kind.
My name is Ollie, what's yours? Do you mind?"
"Grin is my name, my eight armed friend.
Be careful exploring these rocks again."

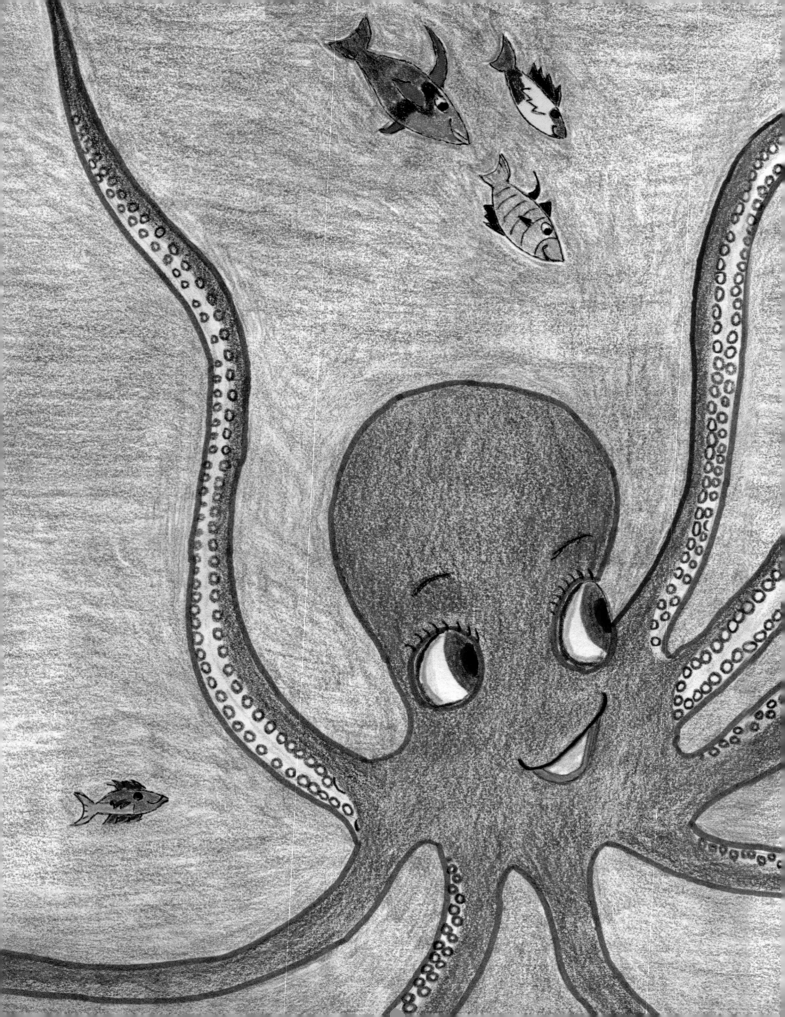

"Grin, what can I do to repay you?"
Ollie asks nicely, if he can help too.
Grin smiles and giggles at Ollie's question.
"Help someone else, that's my suggestion.

Ollie, I feel down deep in my soul,
Helping others is a mighty fine goal."
Grin says to him, again thinking smart.
"When you help others, you tickle your heart."

Ollie swims thinking, "Grin's message is nice.
I will help someone," he tells himself twice.
"OUCH!" Someone cries beneath Ollie's bed.
It's a large manatee rubbing her sore head.

"Pay more attention next time you plop down!"
She shouts and demands, her face in a frown.
"I am sorry I bumped that cut on your face.
I didn't see you resting in this place."

Gazing to the surface, Moo Moo cries, and boats race.
"It's all their fault, they won't slow their pace."
Ollie feels sad, and agrees with her.
"Those creatures should slow down, speed makes
them a blur."

Then little Mee Mee pouts and cries,
And kisses Moo Moo's sore above her left eye.

"I have a plan," Ollie tells Moo Moo.
"I'll make you a bandage for that bad boo boo.
This will work fine, he says without fail.
It's from an old boat-a piece of torn sail.
Wrapping it around Moo Moo's sore head,
He doesn't tie knots, but a red bow instead.

"Be careful Moo Moo, and your cut will heal.
Watch out for fast boats, their blades are sharp steel."

Ollie now wonders, "Moo Moo my new friend,
Do you know the dolphin named Grin?"
Ollie tells Moo Moo how Grin was a big help.
"I too was in trouble, and he heard my yelp!"

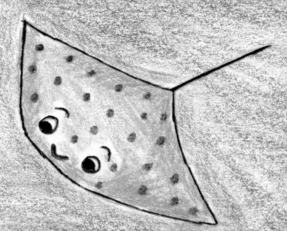

"Grin has a message, and Moo Moo it is true!
Now I understand after helping you.
By helping others, our thoughts become smart,
And the feeling inside will tickle your heart."
"I do believe you," is Moo Moo's reply.
"I will help someone, when I hear them cry."

Moo Moo and Mee Mee swim searching for lunch.
Not for a small snack, but for a whole bunch.
In the sea lettuce, they eat and they play.
But someone needs help, and not far away.
Moo Moo stops munching and crunching to hear.
"Sounds like a dolphin, screeching loud near here!
NO! It can't be!" She shouts and frets.
He will surely drown tangled up in those nets.

Moo Moo swims quickly up to the net.
"It is those tuna fishers again I'll bet!"
"Hi! I am Grin, you kind manatee.
Can you please help? I cannot get free!"

Biting and pulling, the net will not rip.
But someone arrives to help with her grip.
It is Ollie to aid, and by her side,
Together they tear holes open wide.

"Thank you very much for setting me free.
You are both truly special for rescuing me."
Grin says to Moo Moo, and smiles at Ollie.
And Ollie smiles too, as wide as can be,
"I helped out Moo Moo after you helped me."

Then Moo Moo hugs her brand new friend.
"I think your message is wonderful, Grin.
I really feel down deep in my soul,
Helping others is a mighty fine goal."
"I am sure glad that you both agree,
Being helpful is the way to be.
Grin giggles to them both, and Mee Mee too.
Whomever you meet it doesn't matter who,
They need to have friends like me and you."

The End